MY GRANNY'S GREAT ESCAPE

Jeremy Strong

Illustrated by Nick Sharratt

Galaxy

CHIVERS PRESS
BATH

First published 1997
by
Viking
This Large Print edition published by
Chivers Press
by arrangement with
Penguin Books Ltd
1998

ISBN 0 7540 6031 4

British Library Cataloguing in Publication Data

Strong, Jeremy, 1949-
 My granny's great escape.—Large print ed.
 1. Children's stories 2. Large type books
 I. Title
 823.9'14[J]

ISBN 0-7540-6031-4 .

Printed and bound in Great Britain by
Redwood Books, Trowbridge, Wiltshire

CONTENTS

For the Hell's Angel inside us all

CHAPTER ONE

GRANNY AND THE BOY NEXT DOOR

Yurrgh! I don't believe it—my granny's in love! She's at least five thousand years old (well, sixty-two really) and she's gone all soppy about this man next door.

'He's such a handsome boy,' she told me. *Boy!* He's older than she is! Do you know what she did next? She whispered into my left ear, 'Do you think he fancies me, Nicholas?'

I tried to escape, but she clung on to me. 'You've gone very red, Nicholas. You're not embarrassed by your granny, are you?'

1

Embarrassed? I wanted to crawl into a hole and hide. Come to think of it I wanted *Granny* to crawl into a hole and hide.

I'd better give you more details. Next

door to us live a fussy couple called Mr and Mrs Tugg. Mr Tugg doesn't get on very well with us. He's always complaining about something, and Dad keeps calling Mr Tugg 'The Martian', as if he's some kind of alien.

Here is Mr Tugg's general list of complaints:

1 *My dad* Mr Tugg says that my dad is unhelpful, thoughtless and lowers the tone of the neighbourhood.

disgrace

2 *Our garden* Mr Tugg says people should not be allowed to build dinosaurs in their gardens. (Dad tried to make me a slide in the shape of a Tyrannosaurus rex, but he never finished it.) Mr Tugg also says that our lawn lowers the tone of the neighbourhood, because Dad doesn't cut it properly. (I've seen Mr Tugg trimming his lawn with *nail scissors*!)

eyesore

3 *Singing* My dad's got a karaoke machine and he loves singing with it—very loudly. Mr Tugg doesn't like my dad singing on his karaoke machine. He says it gives him a headache.

racket

4 *Our car* Mr Tugg says our car is noisy (true), smelly (true again), doesn't work properly (also true), and lowers the tone of the neighbourhood (possibly).

wreck

As you can see, Mr Tugg is very concerned about the neighbourhood. He's even trying to set up one of those neighbourhood watch groups and he wanted Mum and Dad to help. He came round the other morning to speak to them. He stood on the doorstep looking very important with a deerstalker hat stuck on his head and a pair of binoculars hanging round his neck. (In other words, Mr Tugg *thought* he looked important. My dad thought he looked a bit of a twit.)

'Are you going birdwatching, Mr Tugg?' asked Dad cheerfully.

'Of course not. This is for my neighbourhood watch scheme.'

'Neighbourhood watch?' echoed Mum. 'What's that?'

Dad's eyes lit up. 'It must be when we all watch the neighbours. It sounds fascinating. Who starts first? Shall we come round and watch you, Mr Tugg, or are you going to watch us? Are we allowed to hide? You shut your eyes and count to a hundred while we run away and hide.'

'Don't be so ridiculous!' growled Mr Tugg, and his little moustache began twitching. 'It's not like that at all.

4

Neighbourhood watch means that we keep a lookout for burglars and car thieves and vandals. Why do you think I've got my binoculars and notebook and whistle?'

Dad looked at me in astonishment. 'Phew! Do you hear that, Nicholas? Mr Tugg has got a notebook and whistle! I wouldn't like to meet him in a dark alley.' Even Mum had to hide a little smile.

'It's nothing to laugh at,' snapped Mr Tugg. 'There's too much crime about these days. I've just bought a new car and I don't want it stolen, so I have started up a neighbourhood watch scheme. Everyone else thinks it's a good idea.'

'It *is* a good idea, Mr Tugg,' Mum offered politely. 'Is your new car nice?'

Mr Tugg shot an icy glance at all three of us. 'I hadn't been planning on

5

buying a new car, but if you remember I found an alligator in the last one. I wasn't expecting to find an alligator in my car and I drove off the road.'

(I think I'd better explain. Dad brought a pet alligator home a couple of months ago. We called it Crunchbag, but it kept escaping and one day it slipped into the back of Mr Tugg's car. He went out for a drive with his wife when Crunchbag popped up his head and opened his jaws. Poor Mr Tugg

crashed into a tree. Now he's got a new car and Crunchbag has gone to live in a nearby zoo.)

Mr Tugg said he was planning a meeting about the neighbourhood watch scheme and Dad said he would go along. 'I don't want to be burgled either,' he pointed out. 'The thieves might steal my karaoke machine.'

Mr Tugg bristled at once, which was exactly what Dad had intended. 'Quite frankly, robbers would be doing everyone a great service if they *did* steal your karaoke machine,' he snapped.

'I don't think that's very neighbourly of you, Mr Tugg,' said Dad, trying to look immensely hurt. 'Nevertheless, I shall come to your meeting, but I insist on being given a free notebook and whistle.'

How my dad managed to keep a straight face, I don't know. Mum couldn't. She disappeared giggling into the front room.

Chortle, chortle

7

'Everyone who joins will get a notebook and whistle,' announced Mr Tugg importantly. 'I already have a small supply laid in. Now, there's one other thing I should mention while I am here—'

'Our grass is too long?' interrupted Dad.

'No—'

'It's the wrong colour?'

'What's the wrong colour?' asked Mr Tugg, whose logical brain had now been thoroughly derailed by Dad's off-the-wall questions.

'I don't know,' said Dad. 'Everything probably.'

'What *are* you talking about?'

'I don't know,' admitted Dad with a shrug. 'What are *you* talking about?'

'I was about to say that my father is coming to live with us.'

'Good heavens!' cried Dad. 'I didn't know Martians had fathers.'

'If you were funny I'd laugh,' retorted Mr Tugg. 'My mother died a year ago and he's been getting lonely on his own,

8

living in a big house. He's moving in with us.'

Dad scratched his head. 'Why are you telling us?'

Mr Tugg shuffled his feet and I could have sworn he blushed. 'No particular reason. I thought I had better mention it—in case you think he's a burglar or something.' Mr Tugg tapped his deerstalker. 'That's the sort of thing we have to look out for. Anyway, my father moves in tomorrow.'

Have you put two and two together yet? Brilliant isn't it? Mr Tugg's father is my granny's 'boy next door'! But you don't know the half of it yet!

Mr Tugg senior is sixty-five and he's called Lancelot, although he's hardly a knight in shining armour and he doesn't ride a horse—he rides a big motorbike and sidecar. In fact, he's a Hell's Angel. He has long grey hair tied back in a ponytail and he wears leather trousers

9

and a leather jacket with

written in silver studs on the back. No
wonder Mr Tugg looked so nervous
when he was telling us about his father.

CHAPTER TWO

ONE OR TWO BOMBSHELLS

Big problems today! Mr Tugg's not speaking to Lancelot and Dad's not speaking to Granny.

Apparently, Lancelot has not only moved himself into the Tugg's beautifully neat house—he's moved in his pigeons too! Lancelot is a pigeon fancier and he brought twenty racing pigeons with him and put them in the Tuggs' attic. He was trying to keep them secret but the secret didn't last very long.

Mr Tugg was
polishing
his car
this morning
when Lancelot
let his pigeons out for
a little exercise. Over the
houses they
went, flip-flap-
s p l i t t e r -
s p l a t t e r.
You know
what pigeons
are like,
they're very
messy fliers,
and of course
one of them managed to bomb Mr
Tugg's nice clean
car—**SPLOOP!** 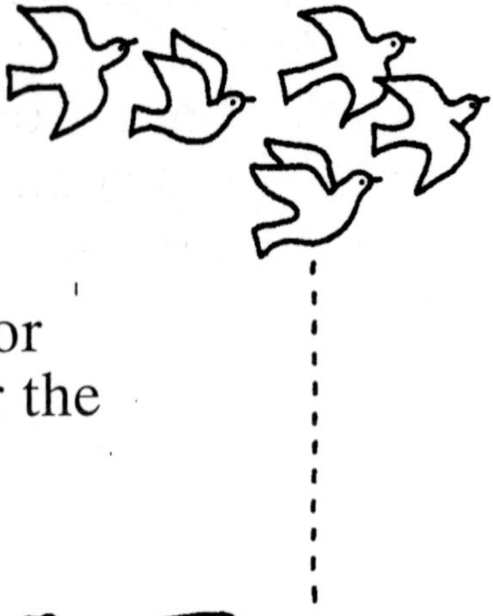 
Mr Tugg went
crazy and hurled
his bottle of polish
after the pigeons.
Unfortunately, he
had left the top
off and most of
the contents

Aargh!

12

lopped straight out and splattered down Mr Tugg's front, which made it look as if he'd been bombarded by several thousand pigeons himself. Mr Tugg went into a full-scale five-star explosion.

Mr Tugg quite often explodes and I have worked out a scoring system:

☆ One Star—Turns red and screws up eyes. Doesn't speak.

☆☆ Two Stars—Deep red colour. Clenches fists and jaw and says 'Grrrrr!'

☆☆☆ T h r e e Stars—Purple. Cheeks tremble. Arms begin to pump up and down. Says things like 'I won't stand for this!'

✩✩✩✩ Four Stars—Face becomes white-hot in colour. Stamps feet. Moustache begins to wiggle violently. Produces a long, loud complaining speech. Often threatens to call the police, the council, the local MP, the Queen, etc.

✩✩✩✩✩ Five Stars—Very, very white and shaking all over. Eyes shut tight. Arms pumping, legs stamping. So angry he can no longer speak. General appearance similar to a volcano or hurricane.

What really sent Mr Tugg into a mega temper-tantrum was watching the pigeon-criminals settle on his own

14

roof and then seeing his own father appear at the skylight going 'cootchy-coo, cootchy-coo'. The pigeons waddled through the skylight and vanished inside. You could almost see jets of steam hissing from Mr Tugg's nostrils and he stormed into his house.

I got the rest of the story from Mum, and she got it from Mrs Tugg. Apparently, Mr Tugg and his father almost had a fight. Mrs Tugg had to calm them down. The pigeons are still up in the attic, but Mr Tugg is so furious he can't bring himself to speak to his own father.

A bit later on, my granny went down to the video shop to get a new snooker video. (She loves playing snooker.) When she passed the Tuggs' house she saw Lancelot's motorbike and sidecar outside. Granny has always liked motorbikes. When she was young she used to go trial-biking with her husband up mountainsides in Scotland and places like that. They won loads of trophies.

Granny was standing there admiring this big black motorbike when Lancelot himself came out of the house, complete with leather trousers and jacket and studs and fringed sleeves, swinging his helmet. He took one look at Granny,

stopped in his tracks and pulled off his shades. 'Wow!' he murmured. 'You're a treat for sore eyes!'

(I ought to point out that I didn't hear or see any of this. This is the story Granny told me afterwards, and it is just possible that she was exaggerating.)

16

'Is that your bike?' asked Granny.

'Certainly is. Want to go for a spin, babe?' (Granny must have misheard him. How could anyone call my granny 'babe'?)

Granny pulled on the spare helmet Lancelot kept in the sidecar, hitched up her dress, and the next minute they were both burning rubber. Lancelot even let Granny take the controls and  he was pretty impressed, especially when she headed for the park so that she could show him some of her old trial-biking skills. However, the park keepers didn't think much of Granny's performance at all, especially when she went hurtling straight through the kiddies' sandpit and then did a wheelie right round the duck pond. (A wheelie with a sidecar? That's what I call impressive!)

The park keepers leaped on to their mowing tractor and gave chase, clattering after the motorbike, mowing

the road and spitting out thousands of gravel pips.

We were sitting peacefully at home when we heard a dreadful roar and Granny skidded on to our drive, leaped from the bike, pulled Lancelot off and dragged him inside. Two seconds later the tractor came clanging and clinking up the road carrying two park keepers, one of whom was leaning out of the cab and wailing 'Dee-doo dee-doo dee-doo!' They thundered on our door.

'There are two Hell's Angels hiding in your house!' yelled park keeper one.

18

'I don't think so,' said Mum. 'I live here with my husband who's upstairs, my nine-year-old son Nicholas, and my deaf mother-in-law. Hell's Angels have not been invited.'

'They came in here— we saw them! We'll search the place until we find them,' shouted park keeper two.

'Excuse me,' said Mum evenly. 'You are not on *Crimewatch* and you are not policemen. Go back to your park and make sure all the dogs are behaving themselves.' (My mum can be pretty cool sometimes.)

The park keepers fizzed and frothed a bit, but they went and as soon as their lawnmower had gone rattling away Granny fell out of the big coat-cupboard in the hall and Lancelot fell out with her.

'You saved our bacon,' grinned Lancelot.

'I think you'd better go home before there's any more trouble,' said Mum.

19

Lancelot Tugg reached out, took my mother's hand and kissed it. 'You're a princess,' he
announced, much to Mum's delight. Then he picked up his helmet, strode out to the bike, kick-started the engine and roared off—all the way next door.

'Isn't he wonderful?' murmured Granny, gazing after him with big doe-eyes. 'He's just like the original Sir Lancelot—a knight in shining armour...'

'He is quite ... nice,' Mum said wistfully.

Dad came down from the bedroom, wondering what all the noise had been about.

'Granny has been on Lancelot's motorbike,' Mum explained.

'It was fabulous,' said Granny. 'We went so fast I thought my dentures would fall out.'

And then came the big shock. I

thought Dad would think all this was great, but his entire face wrinkled up into an angry frown and Dad told Granny he thought she was too old to play about on motorbikes.

'Too old? Play about?' cried Granny. 'I wasn't playing. I was trial-biking. I used to be a champion you know.'

'Yes, Mother, but that was when you were twenty. Now you are sixty-two.'

'That makes no difference at all. I can still ride a motorbike—I *did* ride Lancelot's motorbike, and I did it pretty well too. I even stood up on the seat.'

'Granny!'

'I did, Nicholas,' she grinned. 'I stood up and waved one hand.'

'Mother, I don't think you should,' Dad said sharply.

'Well, I'm going to,' insisted Granny.

'I don't think this Lancelot from next

door is a good influence on you.'

Granny's jaw dropped. She couldn't believe what she was hearing. Mum looked rather surprised too. Granny poked Dad in the chest. 'Are you telling your own mother what she is allowed to do?'

'Yes, I am. You'll only make a fool of yourself.'

'That's a good one,' Mum snorted. 'Really, Ronald! You've made yourself

look foolish more times than you've had hot dinners. You can't tell your mother what to do. Besides, Lancelot is a gentleman and quite charming.'

'He's a sixty-five-year-old Hell's Angel!' yelled Dad. 'Neither of you are to talk to him, do you hear?'

'He said I was a princess,' Mum added coyly.

'He kissed her hand, Dad,' I threw in for good measure.

'He what?' My dad was beginning to sound like Mr Tugg.

'Kissed her hand,' repeated Granny. 'But don't you worry, Ronald, there's nothing in it. I know, because Lancelot and I are going to get married.'

white-hot face

violently wiggling beard

'YOU WHAT?!' screeched Dad, who was now into a serious Mr Tugg impersonation.

stamping feet

'Oh, Lancelot doesn't know yet,' said Granny matter-of-factly.

23

'I have to choose the right moment—
but we will get married. You can count
on it.'

So that's why Mr Tugg won't speak to
his father and my dad won't speak to his

mother. Granny is
head over heels
in love and I
don't   know
what's going to
happen now.
Dad   has
b a n n e d
G r a n n y
from seeing
Lancelot, but I
don't think she will let him get away
with that, especially as Mum's on her
side too.

Isn't life fun?!

CHAPTER THREE

DANCING DINOSAURS

Granny is still going on about Lancelot. It was all she could talk about at breakfast.

'I saw him over the fence this morning. He winked at me, Nicholas. Oh, he *is* handsome! Don't you think he looks like Britt Pad?'

'Britt Pad?' repeated Mum, shaking her head.

'Yes, you know, that lovely actor.'

'She means Brad Pitt,' I explained. Honestly! (My granny is always getting muddled up on things like that. She thinks her favourite band is called Plop. I keep telling her it's Pulp, but she never remembers.) Granny sighed and fluttered her eyelashes.

'Do you think I should ask him out, Nicholas, or is that a bit forward?'

'GRANNY!'

We all stared at her. Dad had to sit

down. Mum put a hand over her mouth. I just boggled a bit. (I'm quite good at boggling. You stick out your tongue and make your eyeballs feel as if they're about to fall out.)

'You can't ask him out,' glowered Dad.

'Why not? How can I marry him if I don't ask him out first?'

Dad collapsed back with his mouth opening and shutting as he fought for words. 'It's not right. I won't have you going out with some geriatric Hell's Angel with a ponytail.'

For a fleeting moment a cunning look crossed Granny's face. She looked just how I feel when I reckon I can trick Mum and Dad into what I want to do. 'A pony?' she said. 'Who's Gerry, and why do we have to know about his pony?'

'You can't go out with Lancelot,' my

26

father hissed. 'He's over sixty. It's criminal.'

Granny smiled cheerfully. 'I had a pony once, when I was small. His name was Black Beauty. He was brown all over actually, and he should have been a she, but I had read the book, and I wanted to call my pony Black Beauty too. He didn't seem to mind.'

Dad got to his feet and stood over Granny. 'Stop pretending to be deaf! You are not to see Lancelot, do you hear?'

Granny glanced at her watch. 'Thank you for reminding me, Ronald! I'm missing my favourite snooker programme on TV. You are a good son to me. See you later.'

She swished out of the room leaving Dad staring after her in stunned silence.

'I think your mother is in love,' Mum said quietly. 'She's fallen for an elderly Hell's Angel from next door. Now what are you going to do?'

'You think this is funny, don't you?' fumed Dad.

'Yes,' giggled Mum. And I have to

admit, it *was* funny.

'That's it,' snapped Dad. 'I shall go and see Mr Tugg and complain.'

This announcement reduced Mum to complete hysterics.

'*You* are going to complain to Mr Tugg? Oh, that's brilliant! That will make a change!'

Dad went striding up the Tuggs' driveway. He rapped on their door so hard he hurt his knuckles. Mr Tugg had hardly managed to open his front door before Dad bellowed at him.

'I won't have my mother marrying your father! I forbid it!'

'I beg your pardon?'

Dad repeated himself while Mr Tugg shoved his hands on his hips and demanded to know what all this was about. So Dad explained. Mr Tugg was rather surprised and the two men began talking. Their voices got lower and lower. Neither Mum nor I could hear a word. This was very unusual. Normally when Mr Tugg and my father talk to each other, their voices get higher and higher and they end up bellowing, as if there's an entire mountain valley between them.

Mum and I crept round the side of our house and were greeted by an amazing sight. Dad and Mr Tugg were whispering quietly to each other and nodding in agreement. NODDING IN AGREEMENT?! They never agreed about anything! What was going

on?

'Quick,' said Mum, 'he's coming back!' Dad crunched up our drive wearing a mysterious smile. Mum stopped him at the door. 'Ronald? What's happening?'

Dad looked at us triumphantly. 'I told Mr Tugg that my mother was not to see or speak to Lancelot. Mr Tugg is in complete agreement and he is going to shut his father in his bedroom until he behaves himself.'

'Mr Tugg can't do things like that to his own father!' cried Mum.

'Yes he can,' said Dad, 'and what's more, I am going to do the same to my mother until she comes to her senses.'

'Ronald! How could you be such a dragon?' But Dad wouldn't listen, and he went off to tell Granny about her doomed love life.

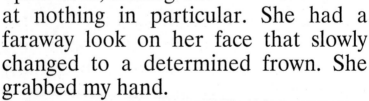

Mum stood at the open door, staring out at nothing in particular. She had a faraway look on her face that slowly changed to a determined frown. She grabbed my hand.

'Nicholas, do you know what we are going to do? We are going to set

Granny free!'

I have to admit that this sounded rather grand. It was getting like some fairy tale. We already had Sir Lancelot-the-Brave and a beautiful princess— well, maybe not exactly beautiful and not exactly a princess either, but you know what I mean. We even had two dragons, namely Mr Tugg and my dad. Mum smiled happily and I felt terribly proud of her.

'We are going to free Lancelot too,' she declared.

To tell you the truth, Lancelot didn't need much help being freed. Later that day, I was up in my bedroom when I happened to glance out of the window and there was Lancelot climbing over our garden fence. He looked quickly all around, zipped across to the Tyrannosaurus rex and promptly vanished.

31

I stood there watching and waiting, but nothing happened. The seconds ticked by. Where had Lancelot gone? Then Tyrannosaurus rex moved—at least the bit of him that Dad had actually finished constructing moved. Staring out of my window I managed to catch a glimpse of Lancelot's face inside Tyro's jaws as the tailless monster tiptoed awkwardly across the grass towards Granny's window.

Have you ever seen a tyrannosaurus wobbling about your garden going 'Psssst!' very loudly? It's not really the sort of thing you expect dinosaurs to say, not even half-dinosaurs. Poor Lancelot was desperate to get Granny's

attention, but she really is deaf, even though it comes and goes a bit.
Eventually he just stood beneath her window shouting.

'Rapunzel! Rapunzel! Let down your hair!'

(This was getting more like a fairy tale by the minute. I think Lancelot must be almost as crazy as my dad.)
Unfortunately Granny didn't hear him—but Dad did! All at once, Dad's karaoke machine bellowed out over the

back garden.

'Don't come a step closer or you're a dead dinosaur!'

Dad was standing at his bedroom window shouting into the microphone and holding a catapult he had confiscated from me. Lancelot froze on the spot. 'Now, take off that disguise and go home. You wait until your son hears about this. You'll be for it then.'

Poor, defeated Lancelot slid out of

the monster and hightailed it back over the fence. You've got to give him full marks for trying. I wonder what he'll do next?

CHAPTER FOUR

I SEE MORE THAN I'M SUPPOSED TO

Things have been quiet for a couple of days, but you know what they say about the calm before a storm. The doorbell rang this morning and when Dad  opened it, he found a giant teddy sitting on the doorstep. Dad walked right round it twice. He even poked it several times, but it didn't move. It just sat there, smiling.

'Where did this pop up from?' asked Dad, completely mystified.

'There's a label on the ribbon round its neck,' Mum pointed out. 'Try reading it.'

Dad let out a groan. 'I might have known. It's for my mother. It's from Mad, Bad and Arthritic next door.'

'It must have cost a fortune,' sighed Mum. 'Lancelot must love her an awful lot.'

Dad shot a furious glance at Mum. 'Get it inside before the neighbours see. I can't think of anything more embarrassing than having a giant teddy bear sitting on your doorstep.'

'What about having a husband who sings very loudly into a karaoke machine, or keeps pet alligators? Don't you think that's embarrassing?'

I kept quiet. I could tell that this argument might get personal and nasty if Mum and Dad weren't careful. I just kept my fingers crossed and hoped they'd find something different to quarrel about. And they did. Getting the teddy bear up the stairs to Granny's room proved to be a major task. The bear was *very* heavy. Mum hauled and Dad pushed and they both came up with quite a few interesting words between them that I can't write down or the paper might burst into flames.

Anyhow, eventually they got the teddy to Granny's room and she was delighted. It was quite pathetic. You

would have thought my granny was about six years old, not sixty-two. 'Oh! It's booful!' She squealed, threw herself at the bear and began covering it with slobbery kisses.

'This is disgusting,' muttered Dad. 'Look at her—a grown granny reduced to a burbling baby. This is really sad.'

'I think it's rather sweet,' Mum murmured.

'Oh, *please*!' groaned Dad in disbelief. 'Fetch me the sick-bucket, quick!' Dad locked the door and stamped back downstairs leaving Granny cuddling her giant teddy and muttering 'cootchy-coos' into its ears.

It was about half an hour later when

we were sitting downstairs having breakfast that I suddenly saw a face go swinging across the patio doors ... and yes, I do mean a face—Lancelot's face to be exact, upside down. He swung slowly from one side of the door frame to the other with his ponytail flopping about, staring at us and making frantic signs at me to pretend I hadn't seen anything. This was a bit difficult because by this time I was almost choking on my toast.

'Are you all right, Nicholas?' asked Mum anxiously.

'Looks as if he's seen a ghost,' Dad grunted.

'I'm fine,' I squeaked, and watched Lancelot swing lower and lower, until I could see that he had Granny's bed-sheet tied round his ankles. She was upstairs lowering him out of her bedroom window! And then the truth hit me like a bulldozer. Lancelot had been inside that teddy! No wonder it was heavy— what a character! He had smuggled himself in and now they were making their escape!

This revelation threw me into a bit of a panic. Should I tell Dad? Should I tell Mum? Should I keep quiet? Lancelot reached the ground, curled himself up and untied his ankles. He got to his feet, beckoned to Granny and grinned as he held the sheet-rope steady.

'Would you like some more toast, Nicholas?' asked Mum.

'Ummm . . .'

'Was that a yes or a no?'

My tongue had locked solid, and no wonder—I was staring at Granny's knickers, swinging around outside the window! She had tucked her dress into the  top of her knickers and now her legs were criss-crossing down the sheet like a big black pair of scissors. I swallowed hard, tried to speak and managed to produce some strange gargling noise— you know, the sort of sound you expect from a deep-space alien when you're first introduced.

'You look as if you've seen something ghastly,' Mum observed, and I thought it was a good thing she didn't know I was staring at Granny's knickers or she'd probably go into orbit herself.

Granny reached the ground safely and untucked her dress. She blew me a kiss and, seizing Lancelot by the hand, she tiptoed away round the side of the house. I was left sitting at the breakfast table wondering what to do.

Dad went upstairs, still being all grumpy. It was very unlike Dad to be so grumpy. Normally my dad is always making jokes and laughing and larking about and driving people mad. I had never seen him so moody. I know he wasn't happy about Granny and Lancelot, but I don't know *why* he wasn't happy.

What was wrong with Granny and Lancelot liking each other? OK, so they were being horribly soppy—but why shouldn't they like each other? I went into the kitchen and asked Mum.

'It's a good question, Nicholas,' she answered. 'You don't remember your grandfather—he died when you were small. He was a lovely man, full of laughter, a bit like your dad I suppose. It was sad when he died. I don't think we ever thought that Granny might one day want to get married again. It's come as a bit of a shock to your father. He thought she was quite happy with us— and she has been happy with us—but now there's Lancelot next door, and your father hasn't got used to it yet. And, of course, you know what your dad thinks about next door! The thought of his mother marrying one of the Tuggs!' Mum began to laugh.

'What do *you* think?' I asked.

'I hope they'll be very happy,' she

said. 'I must admit I'm surprised—but I do hope they'll be happy. Mind you, they've got to escape first, and Mr Tugg and your father won't allow that to happen easily, I can tell you.'

'They've already escaped,' I said.

'What?' Mum grabbed hold of me. 'How? I mean when?'

'Just now, when you thought I was choking. Lancelot must have been hiding inside that teddy. He let down a sheet and they climbed out of her bedroom window and I saw Granny's . . . um, saw Granny go off with Lancelot.'

Mum had clamped one hand across her mouth in disbelief, but now she began to giggle. 'That Lancelot! He's a devil—what will he think of next? To think that we carried Lancelot up to Granny ourselves—what a joke! Now the fat's in the fire! I wonder what your dad will say—not to mention Mr Tugg.'

At that very moment there was a loud hammering on the front door. 'I bet that's Mr Tugg, round here already to complain. Oh dear, here we go . . .'

BANG BANG!

CHAPTER FIVE

WE HAVE BURGLARS

It *was* Mr Tugg, in a three-star rage. (You know, the one where he pumps his arms up and down and shouts 'I won't stand for this!')

'I won't stand for it!' he began. 'Where's my father? What has that scarlet granny of yours done with him? Where are they?'

Dad came hurrying downstairs, wondering what was happening. 'What?' he cried. 'You let Lancelot escape? You fool!'

'He knotted his sheets together. How was I supposed to know that a sixty-five-year-old pensioner would go abseiling out of his bedroom window? And don't call me a fool! I'm not the

45

one with a mad mother.'

'She's not mad. How dare you say my mother's mad?'

'Yes she is mad, and she's deaf too!'

By this time Mr Tugg had reached the f o u r - s t a r level and was changing colours quite nicely.

'Where are they?' he yelled again, and Dad, suddenly realizing that Lancelot was on the loose, gripped the banisters.

'Quick, upstairs—come on—maybe it's not too late!' The two men pelted up the stairs and a moment later Dad had unlocked Granny's door and burst in.

Mum and I waited expectantly.

'No! They've gone! Vanished! Vamoosed! Search the other rooms—quick, they could be hiding!'

Mum and I were just beginning to

enjoy the little drama that was unfolding upstairs when things got even more interesting. A police car pulled up on our drive and  two policemen hurried over to us.

'We've had reports about a break-in,' began the first.

'Someone from neighbourhood watch rang us—said they'd seen two strange people climbing in and out of windows and lurking about.'

'Lurking about?' echoed Mum, and she gripped my hand. 'That does sound dreadful . . .'

The second policeman hurried to the stairs. 'Hey, Sarge! I reckon they're still up there—I can hear them rummaging about.'

'Rummaging AND lurking,' repeated Mum, squeezing my hand even harder in a desperate attempt not to burst out laughing. 'Oh dear . . .'

47

But the police didn't stop to listen.
They whipped out their
truncheons and were
up those stairs
faster

than
the
S A S ,
while Mum
plunged a fist
into her mouth
and had a fit of silent
hysterics. I crept
halfway up the stairs and
peeped. Strange,
frustrated grunts were
coming from my parents'
bedroom and the two policemen were
creeping up on the unsuspecting
robbers.

'On the count of three . . .'

'One, two, THREE! YAAARGH! NOW WE'VE GOT YOU BANG TO RIGHTS! DON'T ANYONE MOVE – GET THOSE HANDCUFFS ON THEM!'

'But . . .' I heard Mr Tugg squeak.

'SHUT UP, YOU NASTY LITTLE THIEVING WORM!'

roared the sergeant. 'Get that bag over his head, constable.'

A few moments later, the policemen came back down dragging two very wriggly criminals with them. Mr Tugg and my dad both had bags over their

49

heads and were handcuffed together.

'Got them, madam!' crowed the sergeant.

'You are brave, officer. Can I have a look at them? I've never seen a burglar before.'

The sergeant scowled. 'They're not a pretty pair, but all right. Take their hoods off, constable. There.'

Dad was speechless with fury. Mr Tugg had gone a very deep purple. Mum stepped back, looking rather shocked. 'Goodness, they *are* scary!'

'Don't worry, madam, they're going to be locked up good and proper.'

'The only thing is,' Mum went on very matter-of-factly, 'that one is my husband Ronald, and this one is our neighbour—in fact, Mr Tugg is in charge of the neighbourhood watch scheme.'

This was followed by a long silence, only broken when Mum politely asked if anyone would like a cup of tea. That did help smooth things over with the policemen, but of course Dad and Mr Tugg were still fuming because Granny Rapunzel and her brave knight had escaped.

My dad wanted the two policemen to hunt the pair down but the policemen said it wasn't against the law to get married, even if you were a thousand years old. Besides, they were enjoying a nice cup of tea. If Dad wanted to find them, he'd have to search for them himself.

'How do we do that? We don't even know where to start looking.'

Mr Tugg gave a strangled cry. 'A clue—there's a clue! I've just remembered—upstairs in Lancelot's room.' He hurried back to his house and a moment later he returned, waving a newspaper. 'Look!' he puffed, and he slammed the paper down on the table. Among all the advertisements was one ringed in red.

HEAVENLY WEDDINGS

For a wedding with a difference why not get married in heaven – or at least up among the clouds.
Take a hot-air balloon ride with your loved one and when you get your feet back on the ground you will be man and wife.
Our balloons leave from Cotman's Field.

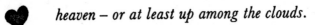

'I don't believe it,' muttered Dad. 'They're getting married in a hot-air balloon—how dreadful.'

'It's not dreadful at all,' said Mum. 'I think it's rather exciting.'

'So do I.'

Dad glared at the pair of us. 'You don't understand at all, do you?'

'Yes we do,' said Mum. 'Your mother and Lancelot want to get married and there's no harm in that. Why shouldn't they? I hope they'll be very happy and I think you're a crab-faced meany-pot to even think about trying to stop them.'

'Stop them!' shouted Mr Tugg, brandishing the newspaper furiously, as if he thought he could swat the balloon from the sky with it. 'Come on—into my car! Maybe it's not too late!'

CHAPTER SIX

MUD AND MUDDLED

We dashed round to the Tuggs' drive, where his new car stood polished and gleaming, even if it did have one or two go-faster pigeon droppings on the sides. We piled inside—and I mean piled, because Mrs Tugg came with us, and she's, well, on the large side. (Imagine a large green jelly with eyes and you're not far off imagining Mrs Tugg, except that this jelly can waddle. Mrs Tugg always wears green.)

Dad called out directions and urged Mr Tugg to drive faster. 'I'm already doing thirty,' Mr Tugg hissed.

'Do you want them to get married?'

'Of course not!'

'Then you'll have to go faster than thirty.'

'Oh, all right . . .' And with that Mr Tugg put his foot down and before long we were doing at least thirty-five.

We reached Cotman's Field just in time to see the hot-air balloon taking off. It was a wonderful sight. The giant rainbow-coloured canopy was rising above the hedges. We could see some people in the wicker basket hanging beneath the balloon.

We leaped from the car and Dad and Mr Tugg went pounding across the field after the balloon, while Mum and The Jelly stood watching helplessly. 'Go on, Granny!' yelled Mum. 'Good luck! Have a good wedding!'

'That's just what I think,' murmured  Mrs Tugg. 'Good luck to them, I say. I don't know why my husband thinks they're being silly. I think he's the silly one. He's the silliest man I know. I mean, fancy cutting the grass with nail scissors . . .'

'He's not as silly as my husband Ronald,' declared Mum. 'Look at him, running about after a balloon, just like a little child.'

'Come back!' yelled Dad, but the balloon was already drifting away faster than he could run. 'Quick, back to the car!' yelled Dad to Mr Tugg, and they came pounding back across the field. Before we knew it they had jumped in the car and gone racing down the road after the balloon, leaving the rest of us stranded.

'I like that,' muttered Mum. 'Typical men—off they go, don't mind us. I'm not going to put up with it. Come on you two.'

'But where are we going?' wheezed Mrs Wobbly-Green-Jelly.

'Lancelot and Granny must have left the motorbike here somewhere and—yes, there it is!'

Without further ado, Mum was sitting astride the bike, pulling Granny's helmet on, and handing me Lancelot's. (I always thought he had a small head.) She kick-started the engine.

'You can't ride a motorbike,' I

shouted.

'Why not? Come on, Mrs Tugg, you get in the sidecar.' The engine burst into life and we charged across the field, with Mrs Tugg bouncing around and making loud squeaky noises, while in the far distance we could see the balloon gaining height. Mum skidded on to the road and was soon racing after Mr Tugg's car.

You can imagine Dad's surprise when we went zooming past at high speed. Mrs Tugg actually began enjoying herself at that point. 'Ha ha!' she yelled back at her husband. 'You old slow-coach! You geriatric tortoise! Faster, faster!' she yelled to Mum, and she beat the side of the motorbike with one hand as if it were a horse. 'Gee-up!'

Dad was furious, and so was Mr Tugg. They came after us and soon we were racing neck and neck. We were even catching up with the balloon. 'I can see them!' yelled Dad, standing on his seat and leaning out of the sunroof. 'They're both on board and there's a vicar with them. We've got to stop them! Get closer!'

Seen close-up, the balloon was enormous and very exciting. The burners roared and spat long tongues of flame into the canopy as it drifted just ahead of us. Granny and Lancelot watched fearfully as we caught up with them. A long rope trailed down from the basket and I had just noticed this when Dad grabbed hold of it. A moment later he was being lifted from the car.

'Stop the wedding—I object!' he yelled and he started shinning up the rope like some crazy stuntman. 'I'm coming to get you, Mother! Double-O seven is coming to the rescue!' And he began to sing the James Bond music at top volume—'Dan-derandan dan-dan-dan, Dan-derandan dan-dan-dan . . .'

Because of Dad's weight the balloon seemed to be having difficulty in gaining any height and drifted away to the side of the road. Mr Tugg almost crashed his new car trying to go after it, and managed to screech to a halt in the nick of time. Mum just raced on, bursting through an open farm gate and into a field, which for some peculiar reason seemed to be full of cars and big, flashy trucks and slogans like MORGAN'S MOTOCROSS written on their sides.

We skidded between parked cars, drove straight across someone's picnic, much to their surprise, and went zooming on with several cheese sandwiches stuck to our wheels and

flapping about like little flags.

A moment later Mum went crashing through some ticker tape and we found ourselves surrounded by an angry wasp's nest of junior motocross bikers, buzzing about all around us. Their chunky tyres sent big flabs of mud flying through the air and in a trice we were splattered from head to toe. Mrs Green-Jelly turned into Mrs Mud-Cake, although she was still just as wobbly.

I could hardly see, and Mum fought to control the big bike among all the little motocross bikes that were swarming about us. Half of them were so surprised to see us that they shot right off the track and ended up buried

in the surrounding bushes.

Meanwhile, the balloon was still struggling over our heads, with Dad hanging on to the rope and swinging backwards and forwards among the astonished bikers like a ball amongst skittles. Every so often he'd go crashing up against some poor kid on a motorbike and send them both hurtling into the undergrowth.

All this might have gone on for hours except that the race marshals brought the race to a halt, leaving our motorbike stuck in a large puddle and surrounded by angry officials, fuming parents and several crying children who complained that we'd cheated.

It took Mum fifteen minutes to explain and meantime the balloon drifted towards the wood, where Dad decided to have a wrestling match with a tree and got tangled up in the branches. The rope twanged taut and the balloon couldn't go any further.

Suddenly the situation was quite dangerous. The balloon was straining at the rope and threatening to crash among the treetops, where the branches would instantly rip the canopy to shreds and the basket would tip everyone to the ground.

Then Sir Lancelot came to the rescue. He climbed over the side of the basket, slid down the rope to Dad and cut the rope free. The balloon jerked clear of the trees and went drifting majestically away, along with the vicar, Granny and the crew, leaving Dad and Lancelot clinging to the treetops.

Granny called to them sadly across the empty sky.
'Lancelot! My brave knight! Come back! I love you!'

'And I love you, babe!' yelled Lancelot.

Mr Tugg drove us home in silence. He got some plastic bags for us to sit on, because we were still rather muddy. He refused to speak to his wife—perhaps he didn't recognize her under all that dirt. I thought Mum might be upset, but she seemed remarkably cheerful.

'I haven't had such fun in ages,' she said. 'And we won!'

'We were disqualified,' I said.

'We won,' nodded Mrs Tugg. She leaned forward and poked her husband. 'And we beat you too!'

Even seen from behind, the ghastly white colour of Mr Tugg's ears indicated that he was going into a five-star rage.

Dad sat strangely quiet in the front seat, staring straight ahead. I turned and gazed out of the back window. Poor old Lancelot—he followed behind on his muddy charger. When we reached home he went straight to his room without saying a

66

word.

Granny wasn't any better when the balloon people brought her back. You should have seen the look she gave Dad. She didn't look daggers—she

looked huge murderous spears—and like Lancelot, she didn't speak. She went upstairs and shut herself in her room.

'Well now,' said Mum. 'I think you and your mother have something to sort out, Ronald.' Dad simply grunted.

I have never known the house so quiet. Granny is still shut upstairs and Dad's sitting in an armchair staring silently into space. The really weird thing is that, even though the house is so still, it feels as if something— *SOMETHING*—is about to happen.

CHAPTER SEVEN

AND DID THEY ALL LIVE HAPPILY EVER AFTER...?

My dad's crazy! He's an absolute zingbat. You'll never guess what happened today—Lancelot and his princess got married! They didn't do it in secret. Sir Lancelot didn't have to steal my granny away. They got married in our back garden—in front of Mum and Dad and Mr and Mrs Tugg and all our friends. It was brilliant! Mum cried, and Mrs Tugg went all wobbly and wept buckets and we all ended up bouncing on the bouncy castle!

Oh yes, I forgot about the bouncy castle. That was Dad's idea. He gets these brainstorms sometimes. You may remember I told you that yesterday everybody had gone all moody and silent. When we went to bed, Dad was still downstairs in the armchair silently staring at nothing in particular, but when we got up this morning Dad was nowhere to be found. There was a note pinned to the armchair.

Gone to find a castle.
Love, Dad

P.S. Tell my mother the dragons are dead.

'What's he on about now?' asked Mum, but I hadn't got a clue.

Later on, there was a knock at the door and outside were two men with something that looked suspiciously like a dead hot-air balloon. ''Scuse us,' they said, and pulled the dead thing through to the back garden. A moment later they started up a little portable compressor and began pumping air into he dead balloon. Mum and I watched from the kitchen window.

'It's another dinosaur,' sighed Mum. 'This must be your father's work.'

'I don't think it's a dinosaur,' I ventured. 'It looks more like . . .'

'. . . a castle,' muttered Mum. 'It's a castle. Why have we got an inflatable castle in our back garden?'

'Because when a princess marries a brave knight they always get married in a castle.' Mum spun round and there was Dad, grinning from ear to ear, and looking just a wee bit sheepish.

'What's going on?' cried Mum. 'What is all this?'

Dad waved his hands dismissively. 'I got to thinking last night— I thought for ages. I thought about Lancelot and how he saved the balloon—saved me too, for that matter. He's a good chap, even if

he does look a bit . . . different. And I thought about my mother and how happy she'd been with Lancelot and how sad her voice sounded when the balloon was carrying her away from him. And I remembered the look she gave me when she got back yesterday. Then I wondered why they shouldn't marry, and—well . . .'

'Well what?' Mum prompted.

'I decided I'd been a bit stupid.'

'A *bit* stupid?' Mum prompted again.

'All right, a lot stupid. Anyhow, I have decided to put things right. So the vicar is coming at twelve o'clock, and Granny and Lancelot can get married in a castle.'

'Dad, it's a *bouncy* castle,' I pointed out.

'I know, Nicholas, but I couldn't get a real one. This is the best I could do.'

Mum ran over to him and flung both arms round his neck. 'It's wonderful,

72

Ronald,' she murmured. 'It's so romantic—married in a bouncy castle!' Then she began kissing him, so I made myself scarce.

Lancelot and Granny were overcome when they realized what was going on.

Mum got out her old wedding dress and it fitted Granny quite well. Lancelot wore his best motorbike leathers. Mrs Tugg picked off the studs from the back of his jacket and then sewed them back on so they said

JUST MARRIED

The vicar arrived and, half an hour later, Granny and Lancelot were married.

Actually, the ceremony was a little weird because Granny's hearing went halfway through the service. The vicar had just got to the bit where he said, 'Do you take this man to be your lawful wedded husband?' when Granny

interrupted.

'Awful shredded hatstand? What are you going on about, you strange man?'

'Just say "I do",' hissed Dad.

'But he asked me about a hatstand, Ron. We haven't got one, have we?' Granny turned to the vicar and smiled politely. 'We haven't got a hatstand,' she explained. 'But you're welcome to put your hat on the table, if you wish.'

Now it was the vicar's turn to look perplexed, and he repeated his question in desperation. Granny lost patience. 'Look, I've already told you to put your hat on the table. If you don't mind I am trying to get married. Do please get on with it!'

74

It was Lancelot who came to the rescue, bending down and whispering very loudly into Granny's ear.

'Of course I take you for my husband!' Granny said crossly. 'That's why we're here! What do you take me for?'

'Then I pronounce you man and wife,' said the vicar with evident relief. 'You may kiss the bride.'

'What bird?' demanded Granny. 'Why should I want to kiss a—ooh!' Lancelot had stopped her from saying any more by crushing her in his arms and giving her a whopping great kiss— a real smackeroo.

Dad got out his karaoke machine and began singing along with all his

favourite tunes and we ended up dancing—bouncing really—all over the bouncy castle—me, Mum, Mrs Green-Jelly, Granny, Lancelot, the vicar, Dad, Mr Tugg—it was great! Lancelot decided to let all his pigeons go by way of celebration, and the pigeons celebrated in the way they knew best—flying round very fast and dive-bombing Mr Tugg's new car—**SPLOOP!**

Granny and Lancelot have decided to go and live in Lancelot's house. It's not all that far away, so we shall still see lots of them. She looked so happy today. She stood arm in arm with her new husband, gazing up into his eyes.

Then she noticed me watching and smiled.

'He really is just like Britt Pad,' she giggled, and hugged him even closer.